"There! Isn't it lovely? What do you say,
Lizzie?" said Mum.

I didn't say anything.

"*Why* don't you ever say anything, Lizzie?"
said Rory. "It's like you've got a zip across your
mouth."

"Lizzie Zipmouth," said Jake, giggling.

A brilliant story from hugely popular, award-
winner Jacqueline Wilson, author of *Double Act*,
The Suitcase Kid and *The Story of Tracy Beaker*.

www.booksattransworld.co.uk/jacquelinewilson

YOUNG CORGI BOOKS

Young Corgi books are perfect when you are looking for great books to read on your own. They are full of exciting stories and entertaining pictures and can be tackled with confidence. There are funny books, scary books, spine-tingling stories and mysterious ones. Whatever your interests you'll find something in Young Corgi to suit you; from ponies to football, from families to ghosts. The books are written by some of the most famous and popular of today's children's authors, and by some of the best new talents, too.

Whether you read one chapter a night, or devour the whole book in one sitting, you'll love Young Corgi books. The more you read, the more you'll want to read!

Other Young Corgi books to get your teeth into:
BLACK QUEEN by Michael Morpurgo
SAMMY'S SUPER SEASON
by Lindsay Camp
ANIMAL CRACKERS by Narinder Dhami

LIZZIE ZIPMOUTH

To Naomi
With many thanks

LIZZIE ZIPMOUTH
A YOUNG CORGI BOOK : 0552 546534

PRINTING HISTORY
Young Corgi edition published 2000

10

Set in 17/21pt Bembo Schoolbook by
Phoenix Typesetting, Ilkley, West Yorkshire

Young Corgi Books are published by Random House Children's Books,
61–63 Uxbridge Road, London W5 5SA,
a division of The Random House Group Ltd,
in Australia by Random House Australia (Pty) Ltd,
20 Alfred Street, Milsons Point, Sydney, NSW 2061, Australia,
and in New Zealand by Random House New Zealand Ltd,
18 Poland Road, Glenfield, Auckland 10, New Zealand
and in South Africa by Random House (Pty) Ltd,
Endulini, 5a Jubilee Road, Parktown 2193, South Africa.

Printed and bound in Great Britain by
Cox & Wyman Ltd, Reading, Berkshire

Jacqueline Wilson

LIZZIE ZIPMOUTH

Illustrated by Nick Sharratt

Chapter One

Do you ever have nightmares? I had such a scary dream I didn't want to go back to sleep. It was just starting to get light. I sat up in bed and looked at Mum. Her hair was spread out over the pillow.

I wish I had lovely long hair like Mum. Sometimes she lets me brush and comb it. I can do it in a funny topknot. Once I put it in plaits and Mum looked just like my sister, not my mum.

I haven't got a real sister. Or a real brother. But today I was getting two new sort-of brothers, Rory and Jake. I didn't like them much.

I was getting a stepdad too. He was called Sam. I didn't call him anything. I didn't like him at *all*.

I frowned at my mum. I took hold of a little clump of her hair and pulled.

"Ouch! What are you up to, Lizzie?" said Mum, opening one eye.

"I was just waking you up," I said.

"It's too early to wake up," said Mum, putting her arm round me. "Let's snuggle down and have a snooze."

"I don't want to snuggle," I said, wriggling away. "Mum, *why* do we have to move in with Sam?"

Mum sighed. "Because I love him."

"*I* don't love him," I said.

"You might one day," said Mum.

"Never ever," I said.

"You wait and see," said Mum. "I think you're going to love being part of a big family. You and me and Sam and Rory and Jake."

"I don't want to be a big family," I said. "I want to be a little family. Just you and me in our own flat."

We had fun together, Mum and me.

We went to
football matches

and we shared big
tubs of ice-cream and
we danced to music.

Sometimes I stayed up really late
and then we went to bed together. I
didn't like night-time because of the
bad dreams.

I dreamt about my first stepdad.

I hate stepdads. I've got a real dad
but I don't see him now. He stopped

living with us ages ago. He doesn't come to see me but I don't care any more.

My first stepdad doesn't come to see us either and I'm very, very glad about that. He was a scary monster stepdad. He pretended to be jolly and friendly at first. He bought me heaps of presents. He even bought me a Flying Barbie. I always badly wanted a Barbie doll but Mum never bought me one. She thinks they're too girly. I *like* girly things. I loved my Flying Barbie but I didn't ever love my first stepdad, even at the beginning.

When we went to live with him he was still jolly and friendly when he was in a good mood but he started to get lots of bad moods. He started shouting at me. I tried shouting back and he smacked me. He said I got on his nerves. He certainly got on *my* nerves. He said he didn't like me. I didn't like him one bit.

Mum didn't like him any more either, especially when he shouted at me. We left that stepdad. We went back to being just Mum and me.

We got our own flat. It was very small and poky and the bathroom had black mould and the heating didn't work, but it didn't matter. We were safe again, Mum and me.

But then Mum met this man, Sam, in a sandwich bar. They ate lots and lots of sandwiches. Then they started going out together. Then *I* had to start going out with them at weekends even though I didn't want to. Sam's sons, Rory and Jake, came too. They didn't see their mum any more. They seemed to like my mum. But I didn't like their dad.

*

"I don't want Sam to be my stepdad," I said. Again.

"He's not a bit like the last one, Lizzie, I promise," said Mum.

I love my mum but I don't always believe her, even when she promises.

"Lizzie?" said Mum. "Oh come on, don't look like that. Don't we have fun together when we all go out, the five of us?"

Mum had fun. She larked about with Sam and sang silly songs and talked all the time and held his hand.

Sam had fun. He laughed at my mum and sang with her and told her these stupid jokes and put his arm round her.

Rory had fun. He played football with Mum and she taught him how to dive when we went swimming and when he couldn't choose between pizza and pasta at the restaurant he was allowed to have both.

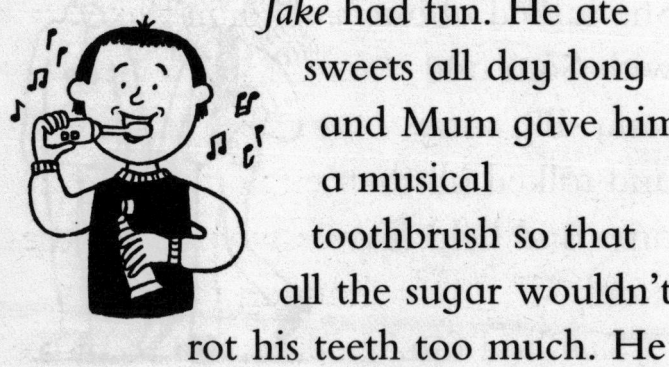

Jake had fun. He ate sweets all day long and Mum gave him a musical toothbrush so that all the sugar wouldn't rot his teeth too much. He brushed his teeth all day long too. He had thirteen Beanie Babies that he carried round with him. They all had to have their teeth brushed too.

I didn't have fun. I thought Jake was a silly baby. And it wasn't fair. Mum didn't mind him having his Beanie Babies. Boys are allowed to be girly.

I didn't like Rory much either. He pushed me over when we played football. I don't think he meant to but it still hurt. And he splashed me when we went swimming. He *did* mean to do that.

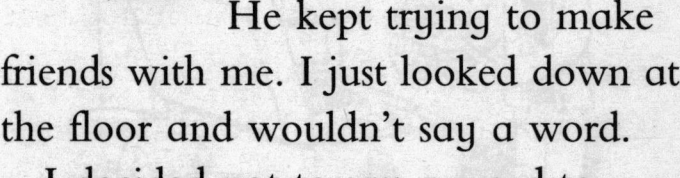

I *certainly* didn't like Sam. I knew he wouldn't be jolly and friendly for long. I was waiting for the shouting to start.

He kept trying to make friends with me. I just looked down at the floor and wouldn't say a word.

I decided not to say a word to anyone.

Chapter Two

I didn't say a word when I had my breakfast. I didn't say a word when I got washed and dressed. I didn't say a word when I packed up my books and my crayons and my stickers and my schoolbag and my washing things and my hairbrush and all my underwear and my T-shirts and shorts and trousers and jumpers and my duffel coat and my welly boots. I didn't even say a word when Mum

threw my old cosy dressing-gown and last year's party dress and my school uniform in the rubbish bin.

Mum said my dressing-gown was all stained and my party dress was so small it showed my knickers and I'd be going to a new school after the summer holidays with a different uniform.

I felt stained and small and different in the car with Sam and Rory and Jake. They came to fetch us and help us with all our luggage.

"It's going to be lovely living in a house instead of that crummy little flat," said Mum. "Won't it be great to have a garden, Lizzie? You can play football with Rory."

"Well, I usually play football with the boys next door," said Rory. "But I suppose Lizzie can join in if she wants."

I didn't want. But I didn't say anything.

"You'll like the swing, Lizzie," said Mum. "Imagine having your own swing!"

"It's *my* swing," said Jake.

"But you won't mind sharing it with Lizzie, will you?" said Sam.

Jake looked as if he minded a lot. I didn't want to go on his silly old swing anyway. But I didn't say anything.

"I don't have to share my bedroom with Lizzie, do I?" Jake asked suspiciously. "Because there's not room. Not with all my Beanie Babies and their special beds."

They weren't real beds. Jake had thirteen shoe boxes with paper tissues for bedcovers. Mum acted like she thought this was sweet. *I* thought it was stupid. But I didn't say anything.

"I've got all my football souvenirs and my rock collection and my worm garden in my bedroom," Rory said quickly. "I wouldn't mind sharing my bedroom with Lizzie but I have to warn her that the worms wriggle around a lot. They *could* just end up in her bed."

I decided I'd mind that very much indeed. But I didn't say anything.

I stood close to Mum. She knew I wanted to share *her* bedroom. But she had Sam now.

"Lizzie can have her very own special bedroom," said Sam. "We can

19

turn my study into Lizzie's room. My computer can easily fit into our bedroom."

"There! Aren't you lucky, Lizzie?" said Mum.

I didn't feel at all lucky.

"I wonder what sort of bedroom you'd like, Lizzie? You can choose the colour for the walls and we'll get you curtains and a duvet to match," said Sam. "What about . . . pink?"

"Pink's a bit girly," said Mum. "How about red, Lizzie? Or purple?"

I liked pink. But I didn't say anything.

Sam painted the walls purple and Mum bought red-and-purple checked curtains and a matching duvet. Sam bought a real little red armchair and a purple fluffy rug.

"There! Isn't it lovely? What do you say, Lizzie?" said Mum.

I didn't say anything.

"*Why* don't you ever say anything, Lizzie?" said Rory. "It's like you've got a zip across your mouth."

"Lizzie Zipmouth," said Jake, giggling. "Can't you talk at all?"

"Don't call Lizzie silly names," said Sam. "Of course she can talk. She's just feeling a bit shy at the moment." He looked round my new bedroom.

"How can we make it a bit more homely for Lizzie? What about your toys? Shall we spread them around a bit?"

I didn't have that many. They all fitted neatly in a drawer. I wished I still had Flying Barbie but she got left behind when we ran away from that first stepdad. I hope she managed to fly out the window away from him.

I wished it was time to leave this second stepdad. He was being jolly and friendly but he'd change soon. I was still waiting for the shouting to start. I was sure he was just pretending to be kind.

I wasn't so sure about Rory. Maybe he really *was* kind. He stuck one of his Manchester United posters up on my bedroom wall.

"There! It's the right colour," he said.

Sam wanted Jake to give me one of his Beanie Babies. Jake didn't want to be kind.

"They're *mine*," he said. "I don't want to give them to Lizzie Zipmouth."

"Hey, stop the name-calling," said Sam. "What about the little purple teddy? He'd like to live in Lizzie's room."

"No, he wouldn't!" said Jake. "He'd *hate* it!"

I hated it in my room too. All that bright red and purple hurt my eyes. I opened up my new wardrobe and shut myself inside.

It was lonely in the wardrobe. I put my slippers on my hands and made them do a dance in the dark but I couldn't think of any other games I could play.

After a while I heard Rory calling for me. And then Mum and Sam and even Jake.

"Lizzie?"

"Lizzie, where *are* you?"

"Lizzie Zipmouth?"

They shouted and shouted and shouted and shouted.

I still didn't say anything at all. I kept my mouth well and truly zipped.

Chapter Three

I got into big trouble with Mum when she found me. She was very, very cross because she thought I'd run away. She shouted at me.

Sam didn't shout at me. I was surprised. But maybe he *wanted* me to run away?

"You made your mum cry," said Rory.

"You're ever so naughty, Lizzie Zipmouth," said Jake.

Mum wanted me to say sorry to everyone for hiding in the wardrobe. I wouldn't say anything. So I got sent to bed without any tea.

I decided I didn't care one bit. But then Sam knocked on the door and whispered my name. He came into my room. I hid under the duvet. I was

sure he was going to shout now.

But he didn't say anything at all.
Long after he'd gone I peeped out.
He'd left a big chocolate bar beside
my bed. Purple to match my
bedroom.

Rory and Jake crept in when they
came to bed at the normal time. Rory
gave me a biscuit. It was a bit
crumbly from being in his pocket. I
didn't say anything but I did smile at
him. Jake didn't bring me any food

but he ran and fetched his purple
Beanie Baby teddy.

"You can have Mr
Purple just for one
night," he said. "Only
you will give him back
in the morning, won't
you, Lizzie Zipmouth?"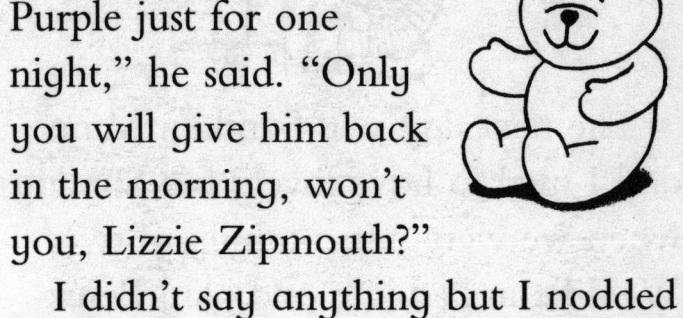

I didn't say anything but I nodded
at him.

I didn't touch the chocolate but I
nibbled an edge of biscuit and cuddled
Mr Purple. Then I snuggled down to
go to sleep.

Then guess what. Mum came in
with a tray of tea for me. I didn't have
to say sorry. In fact Mum said sorry
to me! She gave me a big, big cuddle
and she cried. She promised she'd
never ever get cross again. But as I
said, I don't always believe Mum's
promises.

The next day was Sunday. Mum
and I used to have lovely fun Sundays
when we were just a family of two.
We'd lie in bed late and play Bears-
in-Caves under the bedcovers and
once Mum let me take a jar of honey
to bed with us and she just laughed
when the sheets got all sticky.

Mum liked reading the newspapers
all morning. I liked
drawing on the
papers, giving all the
ladies in the photos
moustaches and the
men long dangly

earrings. Then we'd have a picnic
lunch in the park. We even had picnics

when it was raining. We didn't care.
We just said it was lovely weather for
ducks and went, "Quack quack
quack." Then we watched videos in
the evening. Mum liked old black-
and-white movies and I liked new
brightly coloured cartoons.

We had LOVELY Sundays.

I didn't think I was going to like the
new Sundays one bit. Mum and Sam
had a lie-in. Rory and Jake had
pillow fights and played on their
computer. I sat in the wardrobe. I
wished I had Mr Purple to keep me
company but he was back in his box
in Jake's bedroom.

We all went out to the pub for Sunday lunch. I don't like proper meals like meat and vegetables and puddings. I cut mine into teeny-tiny pieces and didn't eat any of them.

Jake started messing about with his meal too. Sam told him off.

"It's not fair! Lizzie Zipmouth isn't eating hers properly."

"I've told you and told you not to call Lizzie silly names," said Sam. "Eat up at once, Jake!"

"And you eat up too, Lizzie," said Mum.

I zipped my lips shut tight.

"She's a silly baby," said Jake, dropping his forkful of potato onto his plate so that gravy splashed all over Mum.

"You're both silly babies," said Mum. "Oh dear, look at my white shirt! And I wanted to look extra

smart to meet your grandma, Sam."

We were going to have tea with this old, old lady. If she was Sam's grandma she was Rory and Jake's great-gran.

"So does that mean she's Lizzie's sort-of step-great-gran?" said Rory.

I've never had my own great-gran. I've got a granny at the seaside and a gran and grandpa in Scotland but I don't see any of them very often. I didn't want to see this sort-of step-great-gran either.

"My mum and dad live in Australia," said Sam. "So Great-Gran is very special for me."

He said it as if special meant *scary*!

"She's OK, I suppose. But she's very strict," said Rory. "She tells me off if I talk in a slang sort of way. She says it sounds sloppy."

"She says I *look* sloppy," said Jake. "She's always licking her hankie and wiping my face. Yuck! I *hate* that."

I didn't want this old lady telling me off and wiping me. I looked at Mum. Mum looked as if she was worried about being told off and wiped too.

Great-Gran lived in a big block of flats. I hoped she might live right up at the top but she lived on the ground floor. Sam said it was to save her legs. I wondered if they were wearing out. Perhaps they were about to snap off at the socket like an old doll.

Great-Gran looked a bit like an old doll. This strange stiff little lady came to the door. She had very black hair combed so tightly into place it made her eyes pop. She creaked when she bent to hug Rory and Jake. She didn't hug me. She just looked me up and down. She looked Mum up and down too.

"It's lovely to meet you," said Mum.

Great-Gran didn't look as if she thought it was lovely at all.

"Say hello to Rory and Jake's great-gran, Lizzie," said Mum, though she knew I wouldn't.

And I didn't. I stared at the doormat. It said WELCOME. The doormat was telling fibs.

Great-Gran tutted. "Well, you'd better come in," she said.

Mum held my hand tight and we stepped inside.

"Dear, dear! Wipe your feet! Watch my beige carpet," Great-Gran fussed.

But I wasn't watching her carpet. I was staring all round the walls in a daze. Hundreds of shining eyes were staring back at me!

Chapter Four

Dolls! Old china dolls in cream frocks
and pinafores and little button boots,
soft plush dolls with rosy cheeks and
curls, baby dolls in long white
christening robes, lady dolls with tiny
umbrellas and high heels, a Japanese
doll in a kimono with a weeny fan,
dolls in school uniform and swimming
costumes and party frocks, great dolls

as big as me sitting in real wicker chairs, middle-sized dolls in row after row on shelves, and tiny dolls no bigger than my thumb standing in their own green painted garden beside a doll's house.

"Great-Gran collects dolls," said Rory unnecessarily.

"She doesn't collect Beanie Babies," said Jake. "Not even the rare ones."

Sam patted my shoulder. "Are you cold, Lizzie? You're shivering!" he said.

"Lizzie likes dolls," said Mum.

"Well, I'm sure Gran won't mind her having a look at them," said Sam – though he didn't sound sure at all.

"She can look, but she mustn't touch," said Great-Gran.

I put my hands behind my back to show her I wouldn't touch even one tiny china hand.

"These are collector's dolls," said

Great-Gran. "They're not for children."

I nodded. I was very impressed. I thought I was too old for dolls but Great-Gran was very old indeed and she had hundreds. I knew exactly what I was going to be when I grew up. A doll collector!

I wandered very slowly and carefully round Great-Gran's flat. There were dolls on shelves all the way round her living room. She even had three special ballet dancer dolls on tippy-toes on top of her television set. She had a row of funny dolls with

fat tummies on her kitchen window sill and a mermaid doll with a long shiny green tail in the bathroom. The dolls in her bedroom were all wearing their night-clothes, white nighties with pink ribbon trimming and blue-and-white striped pyjamas and soft red dressing-gowns with cords and tassels and little slippers with tiny pom-poms.

"Well? What do you think of them?" said Great-Gran, walking along briskly behind me.

I didn't say anything. But I must have had the right look on my face because Great-Gran gave me a little nod.

"I'd better go and put the kettle on," she said. "They won't have thought to do it, the gormless lot."

I gave the littlest doll one last lingering glance. Her plaits were tied with tiny pink ribbons and she was

holding a little pink rabbit no bigger
than a button.

"I suppose you can stay in here
looking," she said. "But only if you
promise you won't touch."

I did my pantomime of hands
behind my back. But this wasn't good
enough.

"*Promise* me," said Great-Gran.

I didn't say anything but I tried so
hard to make my face look as if I was
promising that my eyes watered.

39

Great-Gran's eyes were a very bright blue even though she was such an old lady. They grew even brighter now.

"I can't hear you," she said. She cupped her little claw hand behind her ear. "Speak up!"

We looked at each other. I knew what she was up to. And she knew that I knew. We looked and looked and looked at each other.

"So you're not going to promise?" said Great-Gran. "Come on then, out of the bedroom this instant."

I looked at her pleadingly.

"What's the matter?" said Great-Gran. "*Why* can't you promise?"

I shook my head helplessly.

"Can't you talk?" said Great-Gran.

I shook my head.

"Of course you can talk if you really want to!" said Great-Gran.

"Open your mouth!"

She said it so fiercely I opened my mouth automatically.

"Aha!" said Great-Gran. "There! You've got a tongue in your head after all. And two rows of shiny teeth. So use them, please, Madam. *Now!*"

My tongue and my teeth started working all by themselves. "I promise!" I whispered.

Great-Gran smiled triumphantly. All the dolls in her bedroom seemed to be smiling too.

Mum called out to me from the other room. I zipped my mouth shut again.

"Don't worry," said Great-Gran. "I won't tell the others."

She put her finger to her lips. I put my finger to my lips.

"You're a caution, you are," said Great-Gran. "I'm pleased you like my dolls. You can come and visit me again. I have some more dolls stored in trunks. I *might* let you play with those dolls if you're a very, very good girl."

Chapter Five

I was sometimes a very, very *bad* girl
at Mum and Sam's place. I'd been a
good girl with my first stepdad. They
weren't going to catch me out again.
Sam couldn't fool me. He'd turn out
to be mean and scary like my first
stepdad. Maybe he'd even be *worse*. So,
if Sam did the cooking I wouldn't eat
any of it, even if it was one of my
favourites, like pizza. If Sam chose a
video I turned my chair round and

wouldn't watch it, even when it was *Little Women* or *Black Beauty* or *The Secret Garden*. If Sam bought us ice-creams when we were out I wouldn't eat mine – not even when it was one of those big whippy ice-creams with strawberry sauce and a chocolate flake. My mouth watered but I didn't even have one lick. The ice-cream  melted and dripped down inside my sleeve.

"Honestly, Lizzie, why do you have to be so silly?" said Mum, sighing as she threw my ice-cream into the gutter.

Sam sighed too. I was *sure* he was going to shout at me this time. But he didn't.

He asked me if I'd like to go over and see Great-Gran again.

"Oh, Dad! Do we have to?" said Rory. "I thought we only saw Great-Gran on Sundays."

"We can't play properly at Great-Gran's. There's nothing to do," said Jake.

"This is a special invitation for Lizzie," said Sam. "Shall I drive you over there after tea?"

I didn't know what to do. I wanted to go and see Great-Gran and her dolls very, very much. But I didn't want Sam to take me. I looked at Mum.

"I can't drive Sam's car, Lizzie," she said.

I still looked at her.

"I can't come too. I have to stay here to keep an eye on Rory and Jake," said Mum.

I looked at Mum. I looked at Sam.

"Coming, Lizzie?" said Sam.

I didn't say anything. I just gave a little nod.

Sam had to strap me into the seatbelt in the back of the car.

"Comfy?" he said.

I gave another teeny jerk of the head.

Sam played music as we drove, silly old children's songs about pink toothbrushes and mice with clogs and circus elephants. Sam sang them all.

"Feel free to join in," he said.

I didn't sing. But my dangling feet did a little secret dance as Sam sang a

song about a tiny house in a place with a very, very long funny name.

Sam took me into Great-Gran's flat but he didn't stay. He said he'd come back for me in an hour.

"She'll probably be bored in ten minutes," said Great-Gran.

I wasn't the slightest bit bored. I had the most wonderful time ever. Great-Gran let me go on another tour round her flat. I looked at the dolls on shelves, the dolls on chairs, the dolls on the window sills, the dolls in their night-clothes ready for bed. Then I looked hopefully at Great-Gran. She looked back at me.

"What?" she said. Her eyes were gleaming as brightly as the dolls.

I swallowed. My voice sounded rusty when I used it.

"Could I see the dolls in the trunk?" I whispered.

"Speak up!" said Great-Gran. "And remember to say please!"

"Please could I see the dolls in the trunk. *Please*," I said, so loudly that I nearly set the dolls on the shelves blinking.

"Certainly," said Great-Gran. "That's a very good girl! Come along then. You can help me get them out."

She kept the trunks in the back of her built-in wardrobe. There were two, one on top of the other. I had to stand on tiptoe to reach the top one.

"Easy does it," said Great-Gran.

I went so e-a-s-y I felt I was in slow motion. The trunk was heavy. There seemed to be several dolls inside. When Great-Gran lifted the lid I saw them lying in a row, eyes shut. They looked as if they were fast asleep.

"You can wake them up," said Great-Gran.

I gently lifted a beautiful big doll with long blonde hair out of the trunk.

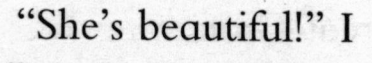

She had a white nightie but no slippers on her pale china feet. Her tiny toenails were painted pink. One of her hands was missing but I didn't mind a bit.

"She's beautiful!" I whispered, cradling her carefully.

"That's Alice. I expect she's a little chilly in that thin nightgown. Perhaps you'd like to find some clothes for her?" said Great-Gran.

The second trunk was crammed with neatly folded outfits – party frocks, winter coats trimmed with fur, sailor suits, checked pinafores, lace-edged underwear, black knitted stockings and little boots with tiny pearl buttons.

My hand hovered hopefully above the clothes.

"Go on, have a little sort through. But don't get them rumpled," said Great-Gran.

I sifted through the clothes with trembling fingers and found a pale blue smocked dress with a white lace collar and a darker blue satin sash.

"Can she wear this one?"

"I think that's actually Alice's favourite outfit," said Great-Gran.

I dressed Alice, moving her arms and legs very gently indeed. The blue sleeves were a little long for her, so her missing hand didn't show. She looked perfect.

Then I woke Sophie and Charlotte and little Edward and weeny

Clementine and got them all dressed up.

"There! Don't they look smart? All ready for a party," said Great-Gran, and she opened another box. There was a little blue-and-white doll's tea set inside.

I thought we'd pretend the party fare but Great-Gran made real pink rosehip tea and opened a packet of tiny round iced biscuits that just fitted the plate.

We were still enjoying our party when Sam came to fetch me home.

"Have you enjoyed yourself, Lizzie?" he asked.

I didn't say anything. Not to Sam. But I nodded so hard my head hurt. When I kissed Great-Gran goodbye on her powdery cheek I whispered, "Please can I come again?"

Chapter Six

I went to see Great-Gran almost every day. I always played with Alice and Sophie and Charlotte and Edward and Clementine. Sometimes we had dolls' tea parties. Sometimes Great-Gran and I had proper ladies' tea parties with big flowery cups and saucers and sandwiches and fairy cakes with pink icing and cherries. Great-Gran let me cut up my sandwich and cake to share with Alice and Sophie and Charlotte and Edward and Clementine.

Once Rory and Jake came too. Rory was polite to Great-Gran but he kept yawning and when he got home he ran all round the garden like crazy, leaping and whooping.

"It's great to be back! It's so b-o-r-i-n-g at Great-Gran's!" he yelled.

Sam said he could stick to Sunday visits.

"What about you, Jake?" said Sam.

"I don't know," said Jake. "I don't like the dolls much. But I quite like the tea party. I might want to take all my Beanie Babies."

I frowned. Jake didn't play with his Beanie Babies *properly*. He got all silly and excited and threw them in the air and made them have fights. I was sure they'd knock the teacups over. Great-Gran would put Alice and Sophie and Charlotte and Edward and Clementine back in their trunk sharpish.

Sam put his arm round Mum.

"I take it you're not into dolls and tea parties either?"

"No way! Though I'm ever so glad Lizzie gets on so well with your gran. I'm a bit scared of her!" said Mum, giggling.

"Don't worry, she terrifies me!" said Sam.

"She can be seriously scary," said Rory.

"She's so frowny," said Jake.

"Well, I like her," I said.

They all looked at me.

"Lizzie spoke!" said Rory.

"Lizzie unzipped!" said Jake.

Mum and Sam were smiling all over their faces. I smiled back. Then I skipped into my bright bedroom to get my knitting. I was making a teeny blue scarf for Alice. Great-Gran had taught me how to knit. She taught Jake too. Jake said he was going to make thirteen rainbow-striped scarves, one for each of his Beanie Babies, but he'd only done five rows of the first scarf so far. I'd nearly finished mine, but I seemed to have dropped several stitches somewhere. I needed to see Great-Gran to ask her to fix it.

We were going to see her on Sunday, the whole family. But on Friday night there was a phone call. It woke me up. I heard Sam on the phone. He sounded very worried. When I peeped out of my bedroom I saw his face was crumpled up the way Jake looks when he's about to cry.

"Oh dear, Lizzie, something very sad has happened," said Sam, coming up the stairs. He put his arm round me. "It's poor Great-Gran."

"Is she dead?" I said, shivering.

"No, she's not dead, pet, but she's very ill. She's had a stroke. She can't walk or talk properly. She's in hospital. I'm going to see her now."

"I'm coming too!"

"No, love, not now. It's much too late. Look, you're shivering. You hop into bed with Mum while I go to the hospital."

Mum cuddled me close and told me to try to go back to sleep, but I couldn't. I kept thinking of Great-Gran lying on her back in a hospital bed unable to walk or talk, just like one of the dolls in the trunk.

Chapter Seven

Sam stayed at the hospital most of
Saturday. Mum took Rory and Jake
and me to football. It was a great
game and our team scored. Rory and
Jake jumped up and down and yelled

and then remembered and drooped
back in their seats, looking guilty.

"It's OK, boys," said Mum, putting her arms round them. "We can be sad about poor Great-Gran and happy about football too. Great-Gran wouldn't want you to stop enjoying the match."

I looked at Mum. I knew Great-Gran much better than she did. Great-Gran thought football a waste of space. Great-Gran thought she was much more important than any football team in the world. She'd want Rory and Jake and me to be sitting quietly in our best clothes at home, worrying about her.

I *was* worrying.

"I want to see Great-Gran," I said.

"I'm not sure they let young children into the hospital," said Mum.

Rory and Jake breathed sighs of relief.

I cornered Sam when he came home that evening. He looked very tired and his eyes were red as if he might have been crying.

"I'll make you a cup of tea, Sam," I said.

Sam looked very surprised.

"It's OK. I can make lovely tea. Great-Gran showed me how. And I hold the kettle ever so carefully so I can't scald myself."

"You're a very clever girl, Lizzie," said Sam. "OK, then, I'd love a cup of tea."

I made it carefully all by myself.

Mum hovered but I wouldn't let her help. I carried the cup of tea in to Sam without spilling a drop.

"This is delicious tea," said Sam, sipping. "Thank you very much, Lizzie."

"How is Great-Gran?" I asked.

"Not very well," said Sam sadly.

"Is she going to get better?"

"I hope so."

"Can she walk and talk yet?"

"She's going to have to learn all over again, like a baby. They're trying to teach her already. But she won't do as she's told."

I nodded. I couldn't imagine Great-Gran letting anyone tell her what to do.

"Can I see her, Sam? Tomorrow?"

"I . . . I think you might find it a bit upsetting, pet," said Sam.

"I know I'd find it upsetting," said Rory.

"Please can I see her, Sam?" I begged.

"Lizzie, it's probably not a good idea," said Mum.

"*Please*, Sam," I said, clutching his sleeve.

"OK then, Lizzie, if it's what you really want," said Sam.

I hugged him — and sent his cup of tea flying. It went all over his trousers but he *still* didn't shout. He hugged me back!

Sam took me to the hospital to see Great-Gran on Sunday afternoon. I held his hand tightly when we went into the ward. It wasn't the way I'd thought it would be. I wanted it to be very white and neat and tidy with nurses in blue dresses and little frilly caps. It was a big strange messy place with sad people slumped in beds or hunched in wheelchairs. One old man was crying. I nearly cried too.

"Are you sure you're OK, Lizzie?" Sam whispered, bending down to me. "We can go straight back home if you want."

I *did* want to go home. But I also wanted to see Great-Gran, though I was very worried she'd look sad and scary now.

"I want to see her," I said in a teeny-tiny voice.

"OK. She's over here," said Sam, and he led me to Great-Gran's bed.

Sam's hand was damp. He seemed scared too.

Great-Gran was lying crookedly on the pillow with her hair sticking up and her eyes shut.

"Are you asleep, Gran?" said Sam, bending over her.

Great-Gran's eyes snapped open. They were still bright blue. But they weren't gleaming.

"How are you today, Gran?" said Sam.

Great-Gran made a cross snorty noise. It was obvious she thought it a pretty stupid question.

"I've brought someone to see you," said Sam. He gave me a gentle tug forward. "Look, it's little Lizzie."

Great-Gran looked. Then her eyes clouded and water seeped out. She made more cross snorty sounds. Her nose started running. She tried to move but her arm wouldn't work properly. She wailed and went *gargle-gargle*.

"What is it, Gran?" Sam said helplessly.

"She wants a hankie," I said. I found Great-Gran's handbag and got a hankie out. "Here we are. I'll wipe your eyes first. And then your nose. And here's your comb. We'll do your hair, eh? It's OK. I'm good at doing hair. I do Alice's, don't I?"

I mopped and wiped and combed.

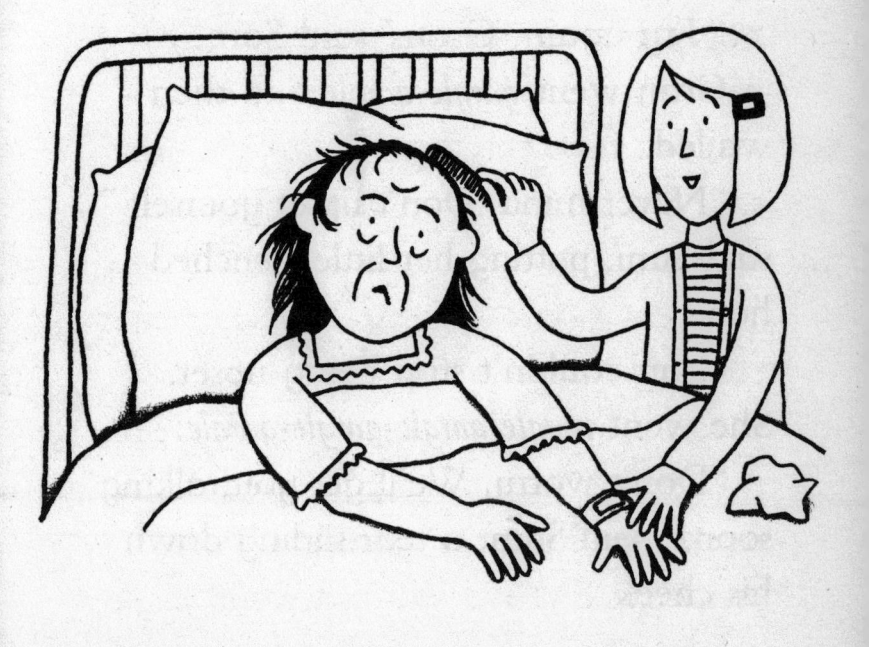

"There!"

Gran still looked bothered, her head on one side.

"Do you want to sit up straight?"

Gran nodded.

Sam helped me pull her up and tidy her pillow. Gran lay back, straight in the bed, seeming much more herself. She looked at me. She opened her mouth. She went *gargle-gargle*, then sighed in despair.

"Try again, Gran,' said Sam.

Gran went *gargle-gargle* and then wailed.

"Never mind. Don't upset yourself," said Sam, patting her little clenched hand.

Gran couldn't stop being upset. She went *gargle-gargle-gargle-gargle*.

"Don't worry. We'll get you talking soon," said Sam, a tear sliding down his cheek.

"We'll get you talking *now*," I
said, taking Great-Gran's other hand.
"Of course you can talk – if you
really want to. Open your mouth!"

Great-Gran opened her mouth.
Sam's mouth fell open too.

"Aha! There's your tongue," I said.
"And your teeth. So use them, please,
Great-Gran. NOW!"

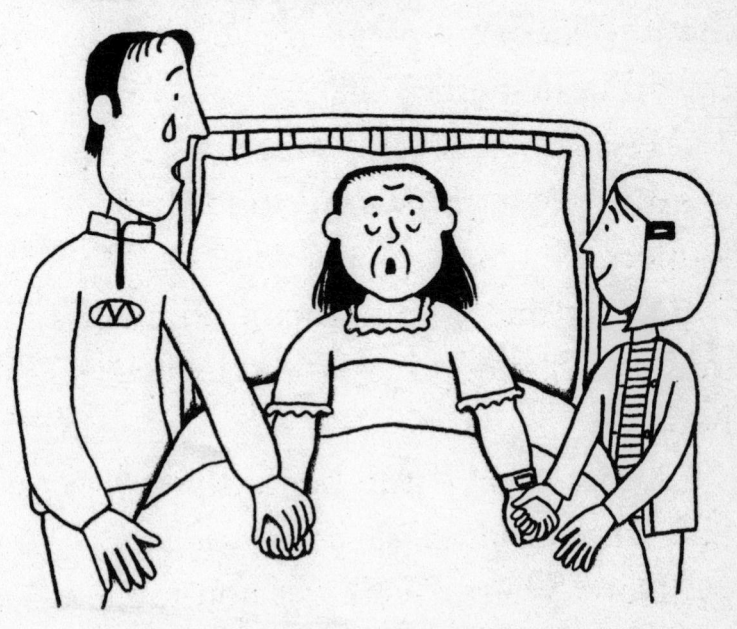

"Cheeky little madam!" said Great-
Gran in almost her normal voice.

She sounded cross – but she held on to my hand as if she could never let it go.

Chapter Eight

Great-Gran didn't die. She didn't get
completely better. She spent three
months learning how to walk again.
She had to use a stick and went very,
very slowly with a bad limp. One arm
wouldn't work properly any more so
for a little while she had to have her
food cut up. I did it for her, very
neatly. I did her hair too and helped
her with her stockings and did her
shoes up for her with
tidy bows.

Great-Gran didn't need any further help with talking though! For the first few days in hospital she got her words jumbled up and didn't always make sense but by the time she was ready to come home she talked perfectly. She talked too much, telling the doctors and nurses what to do. They didn't always like it. Great-Gran didn't care. Sometimes she got very cross indeed and told them just what she thought of them.

"Can't you keep your grandmother under control?" one nurse said to Sam.

Sam rolled his eyes in a funny way to show this was completely impossible. He tried asking Great-Gran not to be so rude. Great-Gran was very rude indeed to Sam.

I couldn't help getting the giggles.

"I think you should try to be

Great-Granny Zipmouth!" I said.

Sam and Mum and Rory and Jake and the nurse all gasped. But Great-Gran didn't get cross with me.

"You're a sparky girl, little Lizzie," she said. "You take after me."

She forgot she's not my real great-gran. But she's definitely part of my family.

She still tells me off sometimes though, now she's back in her flat. I don't really mind. It's because she gets tired out now as one of her legs doesn't work properly. She doesn't like walking very, very slowly with a limp. But she can go very, very fast when she's outside because she now has an electric scooter to get her to the shops and back. Rory and Jake think Great-Gran's scooter is seriously cool. They keep begging Great-Gran to let them drive it but she won't hear of it.

But guess what! When Sam takes me round to Great-Gran's after school, Great-Gran and I sometimes go on secret trips down to the antique centre to see if there are any more dolls Great-Gran wants to buy. Sometimes I skip along beside Great-Gran. Sometimes I get to sit right on her lap and drive too!

We bought a beautiful big china doll the other day. She's got a pink dress and a white pinafore with tiny pink embroidered roses on it. We gave her a tea party with Alice and Sophie and Charlotte and Edward and Clementine when we got her home.

"But she's not going to live in the trunk with them," said Great-Gran. "We'll have to get your dad to build her a special shelf."

My dad? Then I realized she meant Sam.

"He's good at making shelves," I said. "He's made special little shelves for all my mum's CDs."

Great-Gran snorted. She still isn't all that keen on my mum. Mum isn't all that keen on Great-Gran, come to that. It doesn't matter. I can like them both. And Rory. And Jake. And even Sam. Sometimes.

They all like me too. Especially Great-Gran.

"What are we going to call the new doll, Great-Gran? I've got a good name for her! Rosebud."

"No, I've chosen her name already. I'm naming her after someone very special," said Great-Gran.

"Who? *Who?*"

"You sound like an owl! Don't shout! Dear, dear, first you creep around and we can't get a squeak out of you – and now you start shouting at the top of your voice. Calm down. I'm going to call the doll Elizabeth."

"Elizabeth," I said. "Hey, that's *my* name, even though everyone calls me Lizzie!"

"Well, I never," said Great-Gran and her blue eyes gleamed.

I gave her a great big grin, my mouth *totally* unzipped.

THE END